Misty

Wispy

For Brian: the heart and soul of this world we created together.
Thank you for always keeping my head happily in the clouds.
—D.D.

For Rose and our wonderfully wonderful kids
—A.K.

For my mum
—R.B.

All rights reserved. Published in the United States by Random House Children's Books,
a division of Penguin Random House LLC, New York.

Random House and the colophon are registered trademarks of Penguin Random House LLC.

Visit us on the Web! rhcbooks.com

Educators and librarians, for a variety of teaching tools, visit us at RHTeachersLibrarians.com

Library of Congress Cataloging-in-Publication Data is available upon request.
ISBN 978-0-593-18038-9 (trade) — ISBN 978-0-593-18040-2 (lib. bdg.) —
ISBN 978-0-593-18039-6 (ebook)

MANUFACTURED IN CHINA
10 9 8 7 6 5 4 3 2 1
First Edition

Misty the Cloud
A Very Stormy Day

Dylan Dreyer

with **Alan Katz**

illustrations by
Rosie Butcher

Random House  New York

Clare stepped into the batter's box. She looked up and smiled. "Perfect weather for our game! Not a single cloud in the sky."

But there *was* a cloud in the sky . . .
far beyond where Clare could see.

That cloud's name was Misty, and she was a few thousand
feet above the ball field, out over the horizon, in a town
named—what else?—Horizon.

Misty wasn't smiling at all. In fact, she was having a miserable day.

That morning, Misty had been fast asleep, dreaming about happy things—for example, the colorful balloons that often soared up from the earth—when an airplane whizzed by, waking her from her dream.

How rude!

And that made Misty feel, well, a little stormy.

Misty usually enjoyed reading, but today, it wasn't making her feel better.

So she decided to look for a friend to play with instead. *Wispy will cheer me up!* she thought. *He knows how to have fun.*

Wispy was a bundle of energy, always clowning around.

"Hey, Wispy, want to play sky tag?" Misty called.

"I'd like to," he called back, "but my mom says I have to get an early start on my spelling homework!"

"Later?"

"Math."

"After that?"

"Science."

"Wispy!"

"I know. . . .
I'm sorry."

Misty understood. But not being
able to play made her even stormier.

"Oh no! Where did that cloud come from? It'd better not rain on our game!" Clare said. "Go away, cloud. Please go away!"

But Misty didn't go away. In fact, her mood
was about to get even more turbulent.

She went to find her pals Scud and Kelvin, hoping they would play with her.

But Scud couldn't join her for sky tag, either; he had to stay home and help take care of his brother Nimby.

And Kelvin had to get new glasses—the kind with built-in windshield wipers. Very handy for a cloud made of water droplets!

Misty's mood turned unsettled with a chance of rain.
She couldn't help herself—she yelled!
And every time Misty yelled . . .
Lightning flashed! Thunder boomed! Rain poured down!
Today that meant . . .

. . . uh-oh! Game over!

Of course, that made Clare very upset.
Almost as upset as Misty, way up in the sky.

Clare stamped her feet and stomped around the house. She was MAD!

"Misty, what's the matter?" a voice called out.
"Mom, this is the worst day ever!" Misty said.
She told her mother about the airplane,
and how upset she was that her friends were
too busy to play.

"You think that everything has gone wrong, dear. That's made you stormy. And being stormy has made you even stormier."

"Yes!" Misty sniffled.

"Remember, Misty . . . the more you grumble,
the more you'll rumble."

But the rhyme didn't lift Misty's spirits.

"I'm mad and upset, and I'm going to stay
mad and upset," Misty thundered back.

"Forever?" her mother asked.

"Forever!" Misty boomed.

"There's nothing that can cheer you today?"
Misty's mom wanted to know.

"Nothing!"

"Not even those . . .

"... hot-air balloons?"

"Oh, wow! My favorite!" Misty beamed.
"They're so beautiful—and they're coming
this way!"

Misty was cheered by the balloons, and her stormy mood passed. She started shrinking, until she looked like herself again. Even better, her friends floated over.

"Ooh, balloons!" Wispy said.

"Balloons!" Kelvin shouted.

"Balloons!" said Scud as he joined his friends.

"Spoons!" gurgled Nimby, not quite able to say "balloons."

"Mom, look!" Clare said, pointing skyward. "That cloud looks happy again! No more gray sky! No more thunder! No more lightning! Could we go outside and practice?"

"Already got my glove," her mother said.
"Not a storm cloud as far as the eye can see!" Clare exclaimed.

"I predict that the rest of the day will be great!"

And this time, she was
100 percent right.

Some Weather Facts and Fun from Dylan!

HI! I'M WARM AIR!

HELLO! I'M COLD AIR!

I like sunshine and southerly winds.
I weigh less than cold air because
I'm lighter, not as dense.

I like northerly winds.
And I'm heavier than warm air.

WHEN WARM AIR RISES, IT COOLS AND
CONDENSES INTO A CLOUD.

WHEN LOTS OF WARM AIR RISES RAPIDLY, IT COOLS
AND CONDENSES INTO A CUMULONIMBUS CLOUD.

WHEN WARM AIR RISES AND COLD AIR SINKS WITHIN
A CLOUD, IT CREATES STATIC ELECTRICITY.
THAT ENERGY IS RELEASED AS LIGHTNING.

Did You Know?
Lightning is five times as hot as the surface of the sun!
Lightning is 53,540°F.
The surface of the sun is 10,340°F.

Know Your Weather Terms

Turbulence:
Irregular motion caused by air currents

Imagine air in a blender getting tossed and turned up, down, and all around. Then you'd say it was turbulent. When people are in a turbulent mood, their feelings are turned up, down, and all around.

Updraft:
Upward current of air

Downdraft:
Downward current of air

Cumulonimbus (say kyoom-yuh-lo-NIM-bus):
Towering cloud formed by powerful updrafts, often with a head shaped like an anvil. In many cases, it's a thundercloud!

ALL THIS UP-AND-DOWN IS MAKING ME DIZZY!

Static Electricity:
Electric charge produced by friction

In a storm cloud, intense updrafts and downdrafts create static electric sparks in the form of lightning. Remember that blender of air? As the air moves in all directions, it creates static electricity, just as you'd do if you rubbed a balloon on your head and your hair stood up straight.

Little static makes a snap.
Big static makes a clap.

Activities

Count on It

When you see lightning, start counting. Stop counting when you hear the thunder. Divide that number by 5. That's how many miles away the storm is.

30/30 Rule

If you can't count *30 seconds* between a flash of lightning and a thunderclap, the storm is close enough to be a threat. Wait *30 minutes* after the last rumble of thunder before you head outside.

Make Thunder with a Paper Bag

When air near a lightning bolt is heated up, the air is forced so rapidly in many directions that it makes a sound. That sound is THUNDER. Blow air into a paper lunch bag, then close it and pop it. The air is also forced so rapidly in many directions that it makes a sound. You just created MINI THUNDER.